BOOKS BY

PAUL BROWN

CIRCUS SCHOOL

MERRYLEGS

HI, GUY!

PUFF BALL

INSIGNIA OF THE SERVICES

NO TROUBLE AT ALL

CRAZY QUILT, CIRCUS PONY

FIRE, THE MASCOT

THREE RINGS

MICK AND MAC

WAR PAINT

PIPER'S PONY

PONY FARM

Paul Brown

CHARLES SCRIBNER'S SONS, NEW YORK

PONY FARM

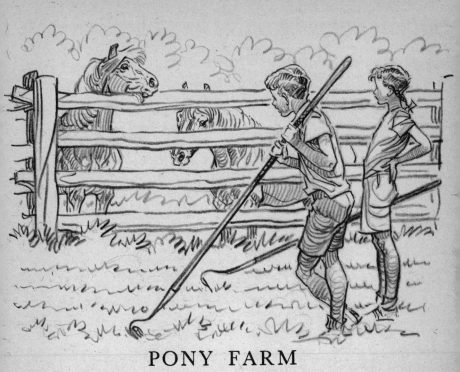

PONY FARM

Grandmother Libby looked out of her kitchen window at Bud and Lynn, not too happily weeding their vegetable garden.

"Mind you get all the weeds, now."

"Oh, Grandmother," groaned Bud, "do we have to weed this old pea patch? We're so tired and our backs ache somethin' awful, and—"

"Now look here," Grandmother Libby said. "You can't be tired. Why, you've only been weeding for fifteen minutes. I know what's eating you. You want to get your legs over some Shetland ponies. Now stop pony-dreaming and watch what you're hoeing. Finish the rows you're on and you can scoot."

Weeds flew and in a jiffy, with whoops and hollers, Bud, half tucking in shirt tails as he ran, and Lynn, her pigtails standing straight out behind her, were streaking on their way.

Grandmother Libby watched them go—the happiest kids she knew—and the luckiest, too, for like all children they were pony-crazy and *they* lived right next to a farm where Shetland ponies were raised.

What a place it is! The minute you turn in at the gate you feel you are entering toyland, because the gay red barns and shelters are pony size. You see little carts and low watering troughs and *everywhere* small ponies are moving about.

The farm spreads out over rolling country broken up into numerous pastures to provide frequent changes of scene for the ponies. This may not seem important to you, but it adds a great deal to the contentment of

the animals to be able to move from one grazing area to another.

A stream which cuts diagonally across the property keeps it well watered. In some fields the brook makes a merry music, babbling and gurgling as it hurries down a hillside. In others, where the ground is level, it stops as if to catch its breath and there it spreads out into glassy pools which mirror the willows, buttonwoods and maples along its bank.

Life at Pony Farm is peaceful and good, but there are anxious times when there is illness and sad times when a pony is sold and leaves for a new home, or a faithful old-timer is laid to rest in the animal cemetery.

"I'm glad it's spring," said Bud. "This is THE MOST

exciting season at Pony Farm. New colts will be arriving every three or four days."

"And knee-high to a grasshopper would almost describe 'em," said Lynn.

MICKEY

As they hurdled the fence into the farm, the first pony they saw was Mickey, the "headman" of Pony Farm. His real name is Matchless Michael of the Titans but everyone calls him Mickey, for short. He is the pappy of most of the colts here and he's a living dynamo of energy.

There he stood, pawing the ground, as he waited for Bud and Lynn to reach him as they crossed the brook by shinnying along the fence rails.

Sometimes life was pretty dull for Mickey with only the company of the old black cat, Joshua, the two guinea hens and the rabbits which live in his corner of Pony Farm. Raising his head and nickering a welcome, he trotted to the edge of his paddock where the brook tumbled under the fence.

He liked to have them visit him because they threw apples for him to chase like a big dog. They'd bring

him sugar and scratch spots he couldn't get at easily.

But, for all his energy, Mickey was quiet and gentle. Either Bud or Lynn could ride him with perfect safety, and they often did to help him let off steam.

SNOWFLAKE

The children were having so much fun with Mickey that they were surprised to find Mrs. Marian, the owner of Pony Farm, leaning on the fence watching them.

With her was Snowflake, the real boss of the ponies —a veteran of Pony Farm for over twenty years. She was a lovely old white mare with a bushy mane and tail and so small she didn't stand much higher than your dining room table.

"Any colts last night?" asked Lynn hopefully.

"Not yet, but we expect one any time now," answered Mrs. Marian. "I wouldn't be surprised if Snowflake didn't set the pace as usual."

Sure enough, towards the end of that very spring day, Snowflake knew that it was time to find her way among the trees to one of the little pony barns. And when the sun came up the next morning she was not alone, for during the night a brand-new colt had come to life.

His fuzzy little topknot had only two ideas in it. One was to stay close up against his mother and the other was food. The first was easy and before long he had found how to get his mother's good nourishing milk.

When his pangs of hunger were satisfied he cocked his little pointed ears, which were full of "wool" and looked out at the sunrise with large blue-brown eyes that shone from beneath unbelievably long eyelashes. His universe, which had been only the shed, began to expand into rolling fields which stretched away to the purple hills in the distance.

"That," said Snowflake, putting her head close to his, "is the great big world in which you are going to live."

DEUCE AND TREY

While the new colt was taking his first look at the world, Deuce and Trey, the farm Dalmatians, were setting out on their morning rounds. They were so named because Deuce had two black spots on his white forehead, and Trey, three.

They darted from bush to fence post, said "hello" to the cows in the dairy herd, scampered among the brood mares and paid a quick visit to Mickey, Joshua and the guinea hens. Finally they came to Snowflake's hideaway, where they quickly spotted the new colt. Their sudden intrusion just about scared him to death, but Snowflake knew all was well. She touched noses with the Dalmatians and didn't object when they cornered her baby and gave him a thorough inspection.

HALF 'N' HALF

The colt didn't fancy these attentions and, to make matters worse, the dogs began to bark.

The noise of the racket carried clear to the ears of Grandmother Libby. It was an old springtime story to her. She wakened Bud and Lynn.

"Into your clothes 'n' be quick. I think a colt's arrived. You can hoe the limas later." In jig time the kids were streaking across the fields.

They didn't take time to cross the brook by way of

a bridge. Instead they skipped across some stepping stones and panted up to join the Pony Farm people who were inspecting the first colt of the season.

"Good old Snowflake. She's done it again," said Pat, the stud groom. "But look at it! Did you ever see such markings?"

"Well, what did you expect? Mickey's *black* and Snowflake's *white*, so-o-o," exclaimed Bud, but here Lynn cut in. "So he's half black and half white. That makes naming him a cinch. Call 'im Half 'n' Half."

"Natch, natch," said Bud, and everyone agreed.

New experiences were coming thick and fast for Half 'n' Half. The big two-legged creatures led his mother away to the main barn and he hobbled along on his awkward legs trying always to keep close to Snowflake for comfort and protection and at the same time to keep her between himself and all these "things."

One scare followed another for the fuzzy little fellow. At the barn, big Pat gathered him gently into his arms and stepped onto a scale, after which his weight was determined by some simple arithmetic.

How much do *you* think he weighed?

Twenty-seven pounds! That's all.

His height at the top of his shoulders, or withers, was only eighteen inches.

Now just stop a minute and think of how small he actually was. Mind you, Snowflake was only thirty-two inches and he could walk under her. He was about as high as the seat of a chair or slightly shorter than either of the Dalmatians.

Cute? He was like a little porcelain figure, and it was hard to believe he was real. He was a very happy colt when his birthday, name, height and weight were entered in the record book and Bud led Snowflake back to the pasture where he could be alone with her.

THE PEST

In spite of all precautions things sometimes went wrong at Pony Farm. A few days after Half 'n' Half's advent into the world, Deuce blocked the path of the ponies which Lynn and Bud were exercising. He barked and darted off into the woods, circled back, and repeated the performance.

"He wants us to follow him," said Bud, remembering stories he'd heard about dogs asking for help.

"I'll bet he'll lead us to where Trey is raising that

steady rumpus," added Lynn, turning her pony around.

When they reached Trey, Bud and Lynn slid off their ponies and peered in among some thick hemlocks. What they saw made tears well up in their eyes.

Bud drew back with an agonized, "Oh, no! Oh, gee, Lynn."

"Go, Bud—hurry—get Pat. I'll stay here and do what I can." There, huddled close beside the still

form of her mother, was a tiny, pitiful newborn filly.

In a matter of minutes, Bud returned with Mrs. Marian and Pat. They wrapped the foal in blankets and took it right into the big house.

Pat brought some mare's milk which was warmed

and put in baby bottles. Lynn was in seventh heaven as she bottle-fed and mothered the poor little waif. "Don't you worry, little lady—don't be afraid. Lynn will take care of you."

Because of the gentle care everyone gave her, the filly quickly learned to put her trust in humans. Of all of them, Lynn was her favorite and the filly followed her every step like a new puppy. With all this attention she soon became spoiled and in no time at all she was a pest.

She dismayed the dairyman by sticking her nose into pails of milk and scampering away when he threw a sponge at her.

"Get out of here, you spoiled brat," yelled the gardener, as she romped over fresh planting to join him.

"Beat it, will you? Go on, scram!" was heard from the tack room where she'd gotten all fouled up in harness that was being cleaned. So—out she scrammed, upsetting a can of polish and knocking saddles off their drying racks in the sun.

She had her nose and feet in everything and so

the Pony Farm people christened her The Pest.

"This has got to stop," said Mrs. M. as she saw The Pest paw a hole in the screen door trying to reach the folks.

"We've got to get her a foster mother so she can use up some of her excess energy running with the other colts," said Pat. "Old Molly is colt-crazy, and if she loses hers again this year it'll be an ill wind that'll blow us good."

And sad though it was, that was just what happened, and the old mare, with a little urging, adopted The Pest and cared for her as though she were her very own.

IN THE PASTURE

Slowly the pasture filled up as one mare after another had her foal. From almost the beginning the little beggars were able to run. At first their gaits were stiff-legged, but they loved to try out their legs racing in circles about their dams.

They nuzzled their mothers for milk and stamped their feet impatiently when it didn't come fast enough.

Grandmother Libby came to spend a lot of time

watching, and she laughed
with the kids when a colt
that was still hungry cornered its mother for a few
extra gulps.

After the runs and the milk they took naps, like
human children, except that *they* went right to sleep.
Stretching out flat in the grass in the warm sunshine,

they'd lie absolutely still, the only movement being the sudden twitching of an ear or the quick slap of a whisk-broomlike tail.

Milk was the mainstay of the colts' diet for months. It was milk, milk, milk and more milk, and any old time was mealtime.

At three days Half 'n' Half, imitating Snowflake, tried cropping a few blades of grass. They tickled his

mouth and he shook his head, but he tried it again.

But it wasn't until they were three months old that he and the other colts learned to drink the funny colorless, tasteless stuff called water. And it was about then, too, that Half 'n' Half and his small running mates began to eat chewy oats and crunchy, crisp raw carrots. They sampled lump sugar and tidbits which Bud and Lynn offered in the palms of their hands. They even tried licking the salt blocks, but it was still milk they liked best.

WIDER HORIZONS

It was a sparrow that first awakened Half 'n' Half to the fact that there were other living creatures in his world besides his mother.

Startled by a movement in the grass

he cocked his head
to get a better look
at it.

He pawed at it

and tried to
pounce on it.

Up went the bird into the air. Half 'n' Half went right up after it. But the bird had flown away.

From that time on, Half 'n' Half began to take heed of other things in the fields. He made a game out of rearing to attack fluttering leaves on low branches, but it was lots more fun to chase birds.

The day he made his prize leap, he'd spotted another "bird." It was a green one this time.

He pawed. It moved. Half 'n' Half pounced. The "bird" jumped. "Gee, this is swell," thought the colt. "This fellow doesn't fly away. He stays and plays with me."

Half 'n' Half was so wrapped up in the sport that he didn't see where he was going. He was absolutely fas-

cinated and—when all of a sudden the "bird" did "fly"
Half 'n' Half went up, then

down—Down—DOWN—KER-SPLASH!

The water gave way beneath him as he went into
it belly-deep after—not a bird—but a frog.

The cold stuff splattered on the colt's back and
splashed up his nostrils, and he got out of there but

quick and scampered to the side of Snowflake, from
whence he peered back questioningly at the spot where
the "bird" had disappeared.

PLAYMATES

Bud and Lynn loved to see how the colts developed from day to day.

They were just like two-legged children in their attempts to get acquainted. After days of peeking and exchanging glances from behind their dams they began to advance towards one another a few steps at a time, only to dart back quickly when they realized they were getting too far away from their mothers.

Then came the time when one ran and another chased him for a few yards. At last there was a cautious touching of noses and then a fast bolt for "home."

Perhaps it was Half 'n' Half's experience chasing birds and The Pest's fun with the Pony Farm people that made them more advanced than the other colts. For as a result they were the first to team up for companionship and play.

Again — just like two-legged brats — they showed

clearly that "three was a crowd" by shunning a third colt which tried to join them.

The mares, too, were like human mothers. Old Molly and Snowflake gave their colts the freedom of the

fields; but another mare, well named Fuss Budget, held out for weeks before she permitted her filly, Brenda, to mix with the others.

Their play progressed from the short, quick dash

stage into the exciting game of follow the leader.

"Boy! See that—Half 'n' Half spun clear 'round when he bucked at the end of that run," commented Bud.

Lynn added her two cents' worth of observation, with, "Brenda and The Pest did it, too; but The Pest kicked straight out with both hind feet right in the middle of her buck when she did it."

Away would fly Half 'n' Half and The Pest, the others following. Some slower ones, like Rosy and Melody, were always left behind. But—when the leaders doubled back they'd fool 'em by turning, too, and getting a head start for the race down the pasture.

"You'd think they'd break their necks—or something," said Bud, speaking his thoughts out loud. "When they go weaving and twisting in between the trees in that bunch of saplings. Look at 'em, will you? Look! Half 'n' Half went between those two trees a mile a minute. Wow! I'll bet he only had a couple of inches to spare."

So it went. A three ring circus all in one field.

As the colts became more venturesome their search carried them farther afield. You could just see what was going on in their fuzzy little heads when they stopped at the top of a steep bank and peered down it.

"You go first," "Not me—you—"
"I dare you," "I will if you'll follow"
was the way the talk seemed to go.
Then, no one having nerve enough
to slide down, they'd all go on with
their racing only to return for another
look at the bank.

Then one day Half 'n' Half got too
close to the brink. The edge gave way

and he went down
with a slide that
ended in a leap-
ing run, making the

wind whistle past
his ears. "Hey—
that was fun!"

The thrill of accomplishment was written all over him as he joined the others but not even The Pest would follow him. That is, she wouldn't try it that day, but after he'd gone down a few more times she joined him in the breath-taking run downhill. Soon all the others were coming down, with slips, slides and leaps, and they all began to look for bigger and better banks and ditches to conquer.

Later their play became very rough and would take on a form of boxing or wrestling. They'd try shoving and jostling and went through all sorts of contortions to prevent the nipping of their forelegs by an opponent. There were no holds barred.

THE BROOK

One day Bud and Lynn pretended that they were cowboys herding wild horses.

They rounded up the mares and then eased the drove to a wide place in the book where Lynn rigged a rope halter on old Snowflake's neck and led her through it. The other mares followed.

Up and down the bank ran the colts, scared by the water, but equally afraid of being left behind. Then one got up enough courage to fly through the water in as few bounds as possible to rejoin his dam on the far side. The others quickly followed.

All but Half 'n' Half. The memory of his dive was too recent. That nasty, cold wet stuff wasn't for him. He just couldn't. As he saw the herd moving away he grew desperate, but he didn't lose his head.

He surely put one over on Bud and Lynn. Racing to a point where the stream was its narrowest, he jumped it. He didn't even get wet.

"Boy! See that! That's thinking things out!" exclaimed Lynn. "Remember a few weeks ago when he

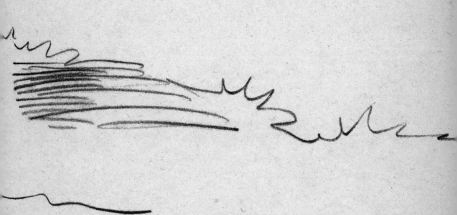

was a little fellow and the flies began to bother him?"

"Sure," answered Bud. "How'd he know to walk under Snowflake, press up against her and rock back and forth to scratch his back?"

"And remember, he'd chase the pesky flies off, too, by walking under low branches and in belly-deep bushes. You can't tell me animals don't reason."

VISITORS

The job that Lynn and Bud liked best was to show visitors around Pony Farm. It made them feel very important and they got a big kick out of seeing the strangers thrill over the things they saw and did.

Charlotte, the sad-looking donkey, and Prince Charming, the big, gawky, hammer-headed dehorned billy goat, seemed to enjoy it too, for they attached themselves to almost every party that started out.

People were afraid that Prince might butt, and

this gave the kids a chance to have some fun.

"Don't be afraid of him. He only wants to play when he rubs his head against you," Bud would explain. "See," and he'd give Prince's hindquarters a hard shove.

That's what Prince was waiting for. He'd stand right up on his hind feet, walk a few steps on them and give a sideways lunge at the nearest person, *but* he'd always stop just before he reached his objective. He'd threaten anyone as the kids took turns shoving him around and the guests felt easier when poor, safe old Prince was left behind.

Half 'n' Half and the other colts, excepting The Pest, felt ill at ease when they saw visitors coming to their pasture. They weren't really afraid, but the things that walked on their hind legs were *so big*— they towered up *so high* above them. They cast uneasy glances at the guests from a safe distance, looking at them with wide-eyed baby stares.

"How do we get to be friends with them?" said a visitor to Lynn.

"Why," she answered, "do as we Pony Farm people do: sit down in the grass. That'll make you 'pony size.' "

So they sat down and soon were surrounded by a ring of curious colts. Step by step they came nearer,

stopping every now and then to look at each other.
"What *is* this?" they seemed to say.

Half 'n' Half came very near. Lynn held out her
hand, and he drew back. Then he brushed his muzzle
against another colt's head, saying something to him.

"Sit quietly," Lynn said, "talk softly." Soon the colts
were letting the visitors put a hand on them.

"Look out!" Bud said. "They'll get fresh!"

And they did! With Half 'n' Half and The Pest

as ringleaders they nuzzled the visitors shirts and nipped them.

"Sit back to back," Bud said. "Don't let them get behind you. They have sharp hooves."

"But aren't they darling?" Lynn said. "Look at their fuzzy little heads and those big eyes."

"When they're a few weeks older *look out!*" Bud advised. "If you try sitting down with them then, they'll nip you good and proper!"

TELLING TIME

By late afternoon everyone at Pony Farm was ready for a rest, but it was then that fresh, deep, rustly straw had to be put into each box stall so that the ponies would be comfortably bedded down for the night.

While Pat and the other hands attended to this, Lynn and Bud dipped wooden measures into a big bin, bringing them out filled with rich, fat golden oats. These they poured into the feed trough in each stall.

Then they looked hopefully at the big clock on the stable tower to see if it was time to bring in the ponies.

But they never had to go into the fields and round them up. By the time they got to the gates at the stable end of the pastures they'd find queues of ponies all ready wending their way across the fields towards them.

"You know," said Bud, "it's as though they had wrist watches on their pasterns to tell time by. How can they be so exact? Every day they hit it right on the button."

"Uh-huh," answered Lynn. "Even daylight saving time doesn't fool 'em. They still head for home at the new right time."

"And look at poor old me," added Pat, who'd walked up behind them. "I have to 'count noses' when I want to go to a certain stall. But not them. They waltz into the stable 'as little as life' and go straight to the proper box. Of course, The Pest pretends to make mistakes, but she knows where she belongs. She just has to stick her nose into places and take a look-see at what the other fellow's got.

"Even the cows in the dairy herd can go to the right stanchion, and let me tell you that's quite a trick. There's them who call animals dumb and say they don't think, but for me—and I've been with 'em all my life—I can tell you they *do*."

PLAYING HOOKEY

"Hey! Hey! THE PONIES ARE LOOSE, THE PONIES ARE LOOSE," yelled Bud, as he dashed for the front door of the big house.

"HEAD 'EM OFF—WE GOTTA," screamed Lynn. "They're heading for the big road."

They took the porch steps in one jump. In seconds they were in the drive facing the oncoming ponies. Bud waved his arms and tried to head off Snowflake, who, with Half 'n' Half, was leading the pack.

First she pulled out the nail.

Then she lifted the wire

hoop, and slid the crossbar.

She swerved and brushed past, knocking him into a heap with Lynn on top of him.

As they untangled themselves, galloping feet thumped by their ears. The stampede was on its way. Lynn rolled over, bracing herself on one elbow, and gasped, "Oh, they're heading right out into the traffic—they'll be killed!"

Pat came streaking across from the carriage house. "It's that Snowflake—she did it again. How she opened *that* gate I'll never know. Why, it had a nail dropped into a hole to keep the crossbar from slipping back. How did she pull that nail with only her lips to work with? I've known lots of horses and ponies that were gate and stall openers, but that little mare beats 'em all."

"I saw them milling around that gate, showing they wanted to change pastures, and that must have been when she went to work on the latch."

That was just what Snowflake had done.

She'd been studying that latch.

After she got the nail out, the rest was easy. She

slid the bar back with her teeth, shoved the gate open and out poured a deluge of ponies.

School was out! They were free. Flower beds and lawns were tramped. After bowling over the youngsters, Snowflake charged at full gallop into the broad four-lane cement highway, the others behind her.

It was a Saturday afternoon and traffic was heavy.

Surprised motorists stepped heavily on brake pedals. Tires screeched and horns blew. A big black convertible roared straight at Snowflake. It was going to crush her to the pavement. But—at the last minute the front wheels caught hold and the car slithered around and almost tipped over.

It was such a near thing for Snowflake that she

left hairs from her long tail in a joint of the bumper.

Snowflake headed east. She wanted to get away from *there* fast. The cavalcade fell in behind. Down the hard road they galloped until a smart driver blocked their way in such a manner as to herd them through a gap in the fence of an old unworked farm.

The soft dirt felt good to their feet and the truants high-tailed it here and there, exploring new country. They surged over the fields and in one quick start, for no place in particular, Half 'n' Half was bumped onto some thin rotten boards which had been laid over an old excavation, and with a sickening crunch they gave way beneath him.

He struggled desperately to stay above ground, but

all of a sudden he disappeared tail first into the hole. Down he slid. The boards jammed about him and he fell slowly.

Where was he going? Fortunately there was only a

drop of six or eight feet and he was unhurt when he
hit the bottom. Half 'n' Half struggled to his feet.
There was just room enough for him to stand up.

It was dark down there and he nickered for his
mummy, but the walls of his prison muffled his plaintive cries.

Snowflake was quick to miss her colt and turned like a polo pony to look for him. He was nowhere to be seen.

Perhaps he was momentarily lost among the others

and she raced after *them*. But—he wasn't there either.

When the ponies dashed onto the main road the screeching of brakes and blowing of horns had alerted the stable help.

One of them brought the station wagon and stopped it just long enough to pick up Mrs. Marian and Pat, who shouted to the kids, "You and Lynn get ponies to help round 'em up. We'll meet you on Hamilton's Hill. They went that way, I think."

And Hamilton's Hill was where the Pony Farm people caught up with the lost herd. They counted noses and at a glance saw that Half 'n' Half was missing.

They were as baffled as poor Snowflake. Where could he have gone?

Poor little Half 'n' Half called for all he was worth, but the tramping of horses and voices drowned the sound of his cries.

Now and then he could just faintly hear his mummy's whinnies. She was so near and yet so far away. He was hungry, too, and to make things worse it began

to grow darker as the sun sank to the horizon.

It was Half 'n' Half's pappy, Mickey, who gave the clue that led to finding him. Mickey heard the colt's plaintive cries and pricked his ears and turned his head towards them. Bud, noticing the slight movement, rode in that direction.

He hadn't gone far before he saw the small black hole in the grass and he dismounted and listened.

Could Half 'n' Half be down there? A nicker answered his thought.

"I've found him. I've found him," he yelled excitedly. "Here he is down this deep hole."

The last words were drowned out by the noise of running feet and shouted questions.

Pat sized up the situation and gave directions. "This'll be easy, because he's so light. Get a fence rail and bring the ropes and flashlights from the station wagon."

"You play you're a deep-sea diver, Bud," said Mrs. M. "You're the only one who can go down that small hole."

"Here—here's your life line," added Pat, as he made the ropes fast under the boy's arms and lowered him into the excavation.

"Ouch! You goat. Hey! Ouch!" floated up to the people on the surface. "Hey! What's going on down there?" they asked.

"Aw, he's stepping on my toes and kicking me in the shins. Doesn't want the rope around him," explained

Bud, his voice sounding far away, and very cross.

When the line was properly adjusted it was passed over the fence rail which had been laid across the opening. In a jiffy, Half 'n' Half was hauled straight up to where big Pat, straddling the hole, could lift him out of it.

"There—that's that," said Pat, dusting off his hands. "Let's head for home and eats. Come on, put back that rail and coil those ropes," and he started to walk away.

"Hey! Hey!" wailed Lynn. "How about Bud?"

"Him? Bud? I thought we'd leave him down there where he can't get into mischief," answered the stud groom. "Sure, we'll haul him out, I was only kidding. You two put a rope on Snowflake and take her home the back way. The others'll follow."

The soft clop-clop of the ponies' feet as they all moved homeward broke the deep stillness of the dark woods. It was a good sound. There was no excitement in it. There'd been enough of that for one day.

They followed the woodland road over a knoll and

saw the comforting sight of the stable lights blinking through the trees.

It was home, and when the ponies, all safe and sound, were munching extra rations of oats in the deep straw of their boxes the kids and all the people of Pony Farm turned to one of Frank's good meals.

Between mouthfuls of turkey with all the trimmings they recounted the events of an exciting day at Pony

Farm until Grandmother Libby said, "Come on. Tomorrow's another day with ponies to exercise and colts to break to halter. It's time that you children 'hit the hay' like the Shetlands."